ORC-US POCUS

LOVE AT FIRST ORC, BOOK 1

AVA ROSS

ENCHANTED STAR PRESS

SERIES BY AVA

Mail-Order Brides of Crakair
Brides of Driegon
Fated Mates of the Ferlaern Warriors
Fated Mates of the Xilan Warriors
Holiday with a Cu'zod Warrior
Galaxy Games
Alien Warrior Abandoned
Beastly Alien Boss
Bride of the Fae
A Sci-Fi Holiday Tail
Monsterville, USA
Monster on Board
(co-written with Alana Khan)
A Monster Worth Fighting For
(Monster Between the Sheets)
Love at First Orc
Third Galaxy on the Left
Monster Mate Hunt
You can find my books on Amazon.

ORC-US POCUS

**An orc science teacher is determined
to give me a lesson in chemical reactions.**

I've crushed on my fellow high school teacher, Thraal, since we first met up in the staff lounge. He's a big, brawny orc, and when he scowls at me through his thick glasses, I pretty much ignite. Sadly, he doesn't realize I exist.

When we're trapped inside the janitor's closet during a Halloween dance, I take the opportunity to show him I'm special. A few spontaneous kisses suggest he might like me too.

Until we're rescued, and he goes back to ignoring me. Well, other than when we get stuck beneath the bleachers or when we're locked inside the field hockey supply shed overnight.

Can I find true love with a geeky orc science teacher?

Orc-us Pocus is a spicy monster romcom and Book 1 in the Love at First Orc Series. Each book is standalone but expect cameos.

Expect size difference, plenty of spice, falling for a co-worker, an awkward, geeky, glasses-wearing orc who loves science and has a creative tongue, laugh out loud moments, fated mates in heat, and a happy ever after.

Love at First Orc Series
Orc-us Pocus
Orc-ishly Ever After
Tinsel & Tusks
Orc Charming
Gaming the Orc
Orc-wardly Yours

Companion Stories
Single Orc Dad

CHAPTER 1
AUTUMN

I stood along the wall in the high school gym, doing my best to chaperone the Halloween dance, but mostly checking out the muscular ass of our high school science teacher, Thraal.

A few years ago, orc males marched out of a previously unknown tunnel on the side of a huge mountain and announced they were seeking mates.

Humans said, okay, sure, we'll give it a try. Treaties were formed, and they now lived among us.

Thraal took a job as the high school's science teacher and started after Labor Day.

"He's so cute," I sighed to my best friend and fellow teacher, Kassia.

Kassia stabbed her finger toward two kids on the dance floor. "Hey, no making out. Megan? Sam? Stop it!" She huffed, sending strands of her strawberry blonde hair shooting up from her forehead. She turned to me. "*Who's* so cute? Because there are a couple of options."

She and I had shared a room in college, graduating with our education degrees seven years ago, and because we were besties, we'd applied to the same school district. Thankfully, Baneroot Academy hired us both.

Kassia taught social studies and world government classes, and I taught math, plus oversaw the Math Club.

"Thraal," I breathed. Per usual, he had a flock of groupies clustered around him, a mix of single teachers and a few students. Also, per usual, he didn't appear to notice their attention. Unfailingly polite and formal (except for his outfit tonight), he appeared oblivious to everyone around him. His steely black eyes scrutinized the room through his Clark Kent glasses.

He was the sweetest guy, completely opposite from my controlling ex.

"You've got it bad," Kassia said.

"Yeah," I said. "Would it be crass to go over and ask him if he's dressed in ceremonial clothing or if the sorta Viking outfit is a costume?"

"Do it," Kassia said, punctuating her words with a nudge of her elbow into my side. She'd dressed as a fairy, complete with sheer wings and a glittery ballerina skirt and bodysuit, and frankly, she looked amazing. Why Jarum, an orc she was crushing on, didn't notice was beyond me.

"I don't know if I dare," I said with a cringe.

"Do it!"

Her low laughter followed me as I started forward, the tulle skirt of my black witch skirt swishing across my fishnet stockings, trying to hold my head steady so my tall, pointed black hat wouldn't slide off my head.

I turned back and scurried over to her, my heels clicking on the wooden Ben gym floor.

"What should I say?" I asked, my voice high pitched and thready.

"Start with hello?" Her gaze locked on Jarum, the school's orc Phys Ed teacher.

"Ya think?" I said with a wry twist of my lips. "It's what comes after hello that I seem to have a problem with."

"You should've stomped over to Wanda and hip-checked her away from him at lunch the other day. Then you'd be past hello already."

I'd started toward him, determined to sit with him while we ate. Talk with him. Adore him from up close. Only to have another teacher claim his attention with a sly smirk sent my way.

"If I fumble my words, he's going to think I've got a problem with social skills," I said. "Give me some tips, oh sophisticated one."

"If I had great social skills, I'd be chatting up Jarum right now."

"Let's make a pact," I said. "I'll go over to Thraal and offer to cast a spell on him." I lifted my witchy wand to punctuate my words. "And you go ask Jarum to dance."

"We're chaperoning. We're not allowed to dance."

"You can help him hold up the wall." He was leaning just like her.

"Alright, it's a deal," she said, nudging me toward Thraal. "Go on. He won't hurt you."

Unlike my controlling ex who'd thankfully had moved to a new town and was leaving me alone.

As I skittered along the outside of the big open gym, lights ricocheted off the disco balls hanging from the rafters, and orange and black streamers fluttered in the sweltering air. The summer heat had held for weeks, and we were all praying for a break. Thunder clouds rumbled on the horizon, but so far, the promise of a heavy rain—and cooler air—hadn't arrived.

Because I knew I'd chicken out if I thought too hard about it, I half-ran over to Thraal. Stopping a few feet away, I swallowed to hold back my sigh of adoration.

The coarse fabric of his dark blue vest shifted, giving me peeks of his medium-green skin. His abs went on for miles, a rugged terrain I'd kill to explore. The intricate gold embroidery on the front of his vest glowed and the fur trim gave his costume a claim-me-now warrior feel.

A leather belt encircled his waist, adorned with silver stars and strapped with both a blunted silver sword and short blade. He wore fur boots and a metal helmet, with the thick golden horns jutting out at his temples.

"Just carry me away and ravish me now," I whispered, my fingers twitching.

His gaze sought mine. Shit, had he heard me? From the way his eyes smoldered as they traveled down my curvy frame, I suspected he had.

Before I could spin and hide my overheated face, he stomped toward me.

"You're in charge of clean-up, aren't you?" he asked in a neutral voice.

So much for thinking he might be eager to ravish me.

"Yeah, why?" I asked.

"Someone spilled punch all over the floor."

"We could call the janitor."

He scowled, never a good sign. "She's not on call, which means you, assigned clean-up, will have to take care of this."

"Okay. I'll get a mop. And a bucket. Water. And anything else I can find in the janitor's closet."

"I'll go with you."

I twisted my lips. "Do you think I'm going to ignore this?"

"I didn't say that."

"No, but you implied it."

He frowned, creating creases on his heavy orc brow. "I'm going with you because you're a tiny human."

"I'm tougher than I look." I lifted my arm and made a fist, but I lost some kick while holding a witch's wand.

Grunting, he crossed his arms over his sizeable chest. "Do you want my help or don't you?"

"I'd be foolish to turn down such a delightful offer."

He grunted again.

"This way." I passed him, aiming for the other side of the gym. There were janitorial closets all over the high school, but the closest one would be inside the locker room.

He followed me to the door and inside, where we passed rows of lockers and approached the door to the closet in the back.

"Inside here," I said, holding up the master key I was given by the principal this afternoon—with a warning not to lose it.

I unlocked the door and stepped inside the tiny room.

Thraal followed, the door shutting behind him.

Three steps took me to the sink where the janitor had left a bucket. Mops and various housecleaning tools hung from hooks on both walls. I turned on the water, added a few squirts of a solution sitting on a shelf, and grabbed a mop, plopping the rag head inside the foaming water.

Thraal hovered behind me. If I stepped backward, I'd brush against him. The thought of pressing myself against his muscular frame made me close my eyes. I sunk into the dream where I rubbed my butt against his rising cock, his arms eagerly wrapping around me. His hands cupped my breasts and—

"Why are you moaning as if you're wounded?" he

asked, his voice low and raspy in my ear. Reaching around me, he turned off the water.

While I was lost in Thraal-land, the bucket had filled. Water sloshed over the lip.

"You're not paying attention," he said in a gruff, grumbly voice.

"Are you always this impatient?" The words popped out of me.

He just chuckled, the husky sound tickling down my spine. "What makes you think I am?"

I turned to face him, my boobs brushing against his upper abs. He was so much taller than me. My five-six to his seven-feet put my lips at nipple height.

His abs twitched, and a vein throbbed in his chiseled temple. Tusks jutted from his lower jawline, and from the moment I met him, I'd wondered what it would be like to kiss his full, dark green lips, to run my tongue along his tusks. I'd grasp his horns and hold on while he . . .

He grunted. "Why do you smell aroused?"

CHAPTER 2
THRAAL

"I'm not aroused," Autumn said with a lift of her chin.

The sultry heat in her eyes gave her away.

I'd noticed Autumn from the moment I stepped inside the school building. She was passing in the hall, her skirt swishing across her ripe ass and teasing her lush thighs. She'd looked my way and froze, her pretty green eyes framed by glorious, long lashes. She'd scrunched her long black hair up into an unkept ball at her nape, and I'd ached to undo the tie and bury my face in the strands. Lick her nape and along her jawline until I could move down across her breasts.

My cock had responded as if I'd found my fated one, but that wasn't possible. She was human, not of my species.

"It's alright if I arouse you," I said. "It's natural."

"Oh it is, is it?" Her arms linked on her chest, and the heat in her eyes was replaced with what appeared to be irritation.

Despite trying to dismiss her from my mind, I kept catching sight of her in the teacher's lounge during breaks, in the afternoons when she relaxed in the library, and while she walked to her vehicle parked in the lot.

I'd held myself back, fearing if Autumn and I tried to do anything sexual, we might not fit. She was tiny and sweet and oh-so detectible. I wouldn't want to hurt her.

Since I'd been here the past few months, however, I'd read online about orc-human relationships. They seemed to find a way.

But I'd still hesitated to approach Autumn

"When a female orc is interested in a male," I said. "It's common for her to bare herself to him. This makes it easier for him to lick her essence, to imprint it in his mind."

"What . . ." She sputtered, shaking her head. "What are you talking about?"

Damn. Had I misread this situation? My heart pinched at the thought that I was indicating interest and she was rebuffing me.

Humans were much too complicated for "dating". As an orc, it was so much easier to grab a prospective mate who openly displayed her arousal, throw her over my shoulder, and take her to a place where we could solidify our mating.

But I suspected that wouldn't work with Autumn.

I dipped my head forward in a short bow. "I apologize. I must've misread. Perhaps I smell the solution in the bucket."

"Way to make me feel good." Her arms flopped at her sides. "We should go clean up the mess."

"Yes," I bit out. From now on, I'd remain far from her. I wouldn't want her to think I was pushing her for something she wasn't interested in.

I hefted the bucket while she eased around me, her side brushing mine and the implements hanging from the wall, making my cock twitch again and the implements bang together.

She turned the doorknob while I crowded close behind her, trying not to slosh the water onto the floor.

She shot me a frown over her shoulder. "The door won't open."

"You're not trying hard enough," I growled, frustration pouring through me. I still smelled something in the air that was *not* the solution in the bucket. But if she denied her arousal, I could not spread her legs and delve inside her with my tongue to verify my suspicions.

Propriety must be followed, we'd been told when we started living among humans. *Do not violate social norms.*

And *do not push the humans when they are not willing, especially related to mating and sex.*

I reached around her with my free hand, my nostrils flaring from her heady scent. The sooner I put distance between us, the better.

I turned the knob.

"You're right," I snarled. "The door's locked."

CHAPTER 3
AUTUMN

"What did you do to the door?" he asked, frowning down at me.

"Me?" I rolled my eyes. "You were the last to enter the closet. Maybe *you* did something to it."

"Of course I didn't do anything to it," he grumbled. "Step aside, female." He lowered the bucket to the floor and tried to ease around me, but tight quarters made me lose my footing and fall against him. I blinked up at him, trying not to focus on his kissable lips. Grunting, he lifted me off my feet with his hands around my waist and placed me closer to the sink. "Remain here."

I saluted. "Yes, sir." My witch hat slid onto my face, and I yanked it off my head, pulling out some hair along with numerous bobby pins and dropped it under the sink.

He frowned. "What is the meaning of . . . this?" He repeated my salute.

"Just a sign of respect, Captain."

His huff rang out, his frown deepening. "I see."

"Are you going to fix the problem you created with the door, or are you going to stand there glaring at me?" I wasn't sure why I felt so irritated with him. Maybe because we were trapped inside a tiny room together. I was trying to keep my heart from flipping over with excitement while he was acting like a grouch.

He wiggled the doorknob and tugged on it.

"It opens outward," I said.

"I know this."

And yet he kept yanking it inward.

"Try pushing," I said, creeping up behind him.

He growled and leaned his shoulder against the door.

"I don't suppose you have a phone on you?" I asked. "I left mine in the teacher's lounge."

"I did as well." He kept slamming his body against the panel, but it wouldn't budge. "We were instructed not to bring them to the dance."

"And you always do as you're told."

His thick brow ridge lifted. "It appears we both do."

"I let loose every now and then." Sometimes. In my dreams.

Let's face it, I did as I was told and avoided stepping out of line. But I wanted to step out of line with Thraal.

He kept slamming himself against the door, and you'd think the dull thuds would call attention, but no one came to our rescue.

"Steel doors like this were made to withstand teenagers," I said to make conversation. "They're tough."

He shot me another raised eyebrow look. "No tougher than me."

"You *are* muscular," I said. "And I'm sure you're tough for a chemistry teacher."

He scowled. "What does my teaching chemistry have to do with strength?"

I shrugged. "Absolutely nothing."

His scowled deepened. "I see." He turned back to the door and pushed hard while turning the knob.

"Maybe step back and rush into it?" I said.

"We have no battering ram."

"You mean like a tree?"

"Yes, like a tree."

"No one does that outside of historical novels and reenactments, do they?"

"Where I come from, it isn't uncommon."

"I thought you lived in town."

"I do," he growled, slamming his shoulder against the unbudging door.

I squinted around inside the closet. "I don't see a tree, so we're out of battering rams at the moment."

He huffed and kept slamming himself against the door. Finally, he stopped and turned, leaning against the panel.

"Your cheeks are flushed," I said.

"I don't blush."

"I meant from your exertion."

"Female, I can battle an entire day without breaking a sweat."

"I bet that earns you brownie points on dates," I said with a smirk.

"Points are often awarded."

My low chuckle rang out. He was misunderstanding, but I wasn't going to correct him. It was time to thrust aside my snarky attitude and take this chance for a normal conversation.

"What are we going to do?" I asked.

"We'll periodically bang on the door. Someone will hear and open it from the other side."

"That's wise."

His gaze narrowed on my face. He must think I was being sarcastic, but I wasn't. He'd impressed me from the moment I met him and not just because of his amazing physical appearance. The insightful questions he'd asked during orientation week told me he was smart. Everything I'd heard since then only reinforced my opinion.

I leaned against the wall, making the brooms and other cleaning implements jangle together.

We waited, him periodically smacking the door with a pipe he found leaning in the corner.

Eventually, I sat on the concrete floor, drawing my knees up because I was chilly.

"We've been here at least an hour," I finally said after checking my watch. "The dance is ending soon. Someone should hear us."

He nodded and banged again. He kept it up for another hour to the point where my ears were ringing. Finally, he returned the pipe to the corner where he'd found it.

"No one's going to hear us tonight," I said. "Tomorrow's Saturday. Do you know if the janitor comes in on weekends?"

"Not any longer. Budget cuts, remember? They told us we need to empty our own trash at the end of the week."

"Yeah, that's right." Fear tiptoed through my veins. "Do you think we'll be here all weekend?"

"I hope not," he said, sitting across from me. Because of our cramped quarters, he couldn't stretch his legs out fully.

"I've got this," I said, pulling a protein bar from my pocket. "We can share it."

"It's clever of you to carry one with you at all times."

"Sometimes, I get the munchies. I'm trying to watch carbs, and this fills me up."

"You'll eat it, then."

"I'll share it," I said.

"I won't consume your food, little human."

"Why do you call me that?" I asked.

His gaze drifted down my body. "Isn't it obvious? You're tiny. Puny. Defenseless. Human."

"I took karate once." I lifted my arm, making a fist to show off my muscle. "I might surprise you one of these days."

The hint of a smile tugged on his lips before he smoothed them.

"Better watch out," I said.

"Because you know this karate?"

"I meant that almost-smile. Keep it up and it might stick."

"I smile," he grumbled.

I tilted my head. He had the most expressive eyes. You'd think being darker than pitch, they'd reveal nothing. But just like the deepest night, when the moon hid her face, the world's true beauty shone through; his gave me hints. "I'm not sure I've seen you smile before."

He stretched his lips, revealing his even teeth and two-inch tusks. "See? A smile."

"What would it take for you to smile fully? You know the kind. The one where your heart is fully into it."

"I'm not sure I can."

"Try," I said, nudging him with the tip of my pointy black witch shoe. It curled up over the toes, and I'd adored them from the moment I saw them. I was contemplating wearing them to school if I could get away with it. "Show me what a true smile looks like on Thraal."

His gaze fell to my lips, and for a second, I thought he'd

ignore my dare. Then his lips lifted in a smile that made my heart seize.

I tried to swallow past the lump of joy in my throat. "That's a good smile." My voice came out husky. "I like it."

CHAPTER 4

THRAAL

Time passed.

Autumn released a shiver. The concrete floor was chilling her to the bone.

I dropped my legs, lifting my heels onto the wall beside her and patted my thighs. "Sit here."

Her eyes widened, and while she could be shocked, perhaps thinking I was being impertinent, a swirl of lust in the pretty green depths told me otherwise.

Did she like me?

I'd craved her from almost the moment we met, but I'd never suspected my feelings could be more than one-sided.

That same sweet smell I'd caught lifting off her skin earlier floated around me once more.

She *was* aroused.

My heart flopped behind my ribs, but I told it to stand down.

"You mean sit on your lap?" she gulped out.

"You're cold. Orcs are warm all the time." Her gaze narrowed on my face. "I promise this is an offer in friendship."

She grunted as she crawled over and perched her sweet little ass on my thighs. "Only friendship?"

I froze, unsure what to say to that.

"Never mind," she said, her puff of air making her black bangs shoot up off her forehead.

"I'm going to put my arms around you," I said.

She leaned back against my chest. "Wow. You really are warm. How is that possible?"

Because she excited me.

When she wiggled around to face me and sunk fully against my body, my cock stirred. I started internally running through the periodic table.

When she put her arms around me, my groan of desire slipped out.

Leaning back in my arms, she peered up at me. "Are you okay?"

"The Law of Conservation of Mass states that in a closed system, the total mass of the reactants must be equal to the total mass of the products."

She frowned. "Are you sure?"

"I am."

The sparkle in her eyes gave away her amusement. With a few more wiggles, she straddled my waist, her heels at my back. "When I'm stressed, I go through the math law of nine."

"What makes you believe I'm stressed?"

Her head tilted. "Aren't you?"

"Maybe . . ." I pinched my eyes shut. Should I mention this or hope she didn't notice? "Maybe I'm excited about something."

"Since it's not us being trapped in the janitor's closet for the weekend with only one protein bar, what could you be excited about?" The realization dawned on her face, and she stilled. "You leaned the pipe in the corner."

"You're correct."

"So why is there a pipe in your pants?"

CHAPTER 5
AUTUMN

I held up my hand. "Wait. I know. Your stiff cock is the natural reaction to a woman sitting on your lap. It has nothing to do with me."

"What if it did?"

I frowned. "Well . . . I don't know what to say to that."

His head lowered to be level with mine, and his smoldering gaze landed on my mouth.

Oh, boy. My heart fluttered and my pulse rocketed into outer space.

"Yes or no?" he barked.

"Um . . . sure."

He slanted his lips across mine. His tusks were hard, but in a good way, pressing against my bottom lip.

Sparks shot through me, centering in my core. I rubbed my groin against his, loving how hard and big he was.

His arms tightened around me, and his growl rumbled in his chest.

I'd died and gone to heaven—or Valhalla, in my Viking-dressed orc's case.

His hands bunched up my skirt, and he ran his palms

across my thighs, rubbing deeply, gradually moving toward my core.

When he stroked my clit through my panties, I hissed, breaking our kiss.

He stared down at me, his eyes locked with mine as he rubbed my clit. "You're wet."

I could only nod.

"I'm going to make you wetter," he growled, pressing harder, creating circles that sent shockwaves through my bones.

I rocked against his hand shamelessly, my body quivering already. I was going to explode from his simple touch. Somehow, our squabbles and snarky conversation had triggered need inside me, one only Thraal could satisfy.

While his thumb remained locked on my clit, he shoved aside my saturated panties with his other hand and pushed a finger inside me.

My moan ripped from me.

"Not wet enough," he said. "Can I make you wetter, little human?"

My head was jerking up and down like a bobblehead doll mounted on his thighs.

I rode his finger as he pushed it deep inside me, dragging it out while swirling it around to hit every inch of my inner walls.

My body sucked on his finger, and when he slipped a few more inside me, still rubbing my clit, I groaned.

"Getting there," he said softly, kissing along my jawline to my ear. "I want you wetter for me. So wet you drench the front of my pants and your thighs."

Under any other circumstances, I'd cringe. I was shy about my sexuality. I'd only been with a few guys. But the thought of saturating the front of his pants with the evidence of my desire made me lift and drop back down on his coiled fingers.

"Ride my hand," he said. "Ride me like there's no tomorrow. No today. Like there's only this moment and you finding your pleasure."

I clutched his shoulders, jerking my hips against him, bouncing up and down as I roared toward my release.

"I want to watch you come," he whispered. "Will you give that to me?"

"Yes. Yes!"

My guttural gasp rocketed throughout the room as my body soared toward the peak. I yanked on his fur vest, trembling as warmth surged through my veins. I was blasting across the universe on a one-way course toward something I'd never felt before.

His ragged breathing echoed around us, intensifying every pulse of delight shooting through me.

I could smell my arousal, a salty, sweet, musky scent lingering in the air, and the wet, frantic sounds of my body seeking bliss made me move faster. I rode each crest, climbing higher.

His lips pressed against mine in a hard kiss, our tongues twisting together. My heart pounded so fast it might shoot from my chest.

His fingers pushed deeper inside me, twisting and stroking, while his thumb ground against my clit.

"Come, Autumn," he snarled. "It's mine and I'm greedy. I want to hear you scream."

My eyelids fluttered, and I tipped my head back as I slammed down onto his thick fingers.

He watched me, his eyes smoldering.

"I'm gonna . . ." My words dissolved into nothing. I

could barely think. "I'm greedy, too," I growled. "I want your big, thick cock buried inside me."

"No." His lips curled up briefly in a devilish smile. "Not yet."

"Please," I keened. "Push it inside me."

"Like this?" He added the rest of his fingers, making a thick, long band pumping within me as I dropped down onto it. His other hand pinched my clit, rolling it.

"Ah! Yes. More."

"You *are* greedy, little one. Take what I have to offer."

I wanted it all, but I was too far gone to care about anything but his thick weave of fingers driving inside me.

Stroking his muscular chest, I gave way, roaring through an orgasm as if I slammed through a concrete wall.

CHAPTER 6

THRAAL

Before I could say anything, the sound of a key in the door rang out.

Autumn's panic-filled gaze met mine. She slid off my fingers, her body making a sucking sound that was going to haunt me for the rest of my days.

She scrambled to her feet and straightened her clothing, not looking my way.

Was she upset it happened or did she want something more? I couldn't tell from her expression. Humans were hard to figure out.

One thing was clear, however. She was tiny compared to me, and if we had sex, I'd split her apart. She'd taken my fingers, but my cock was bigger.

If we took things further, it was going to be a challenge to get inside her. Assuming she wanted more. I'd take my cue from her behavior.

I rose as the door opened and the janitor bustled inside the tiny room. Maryanne paused and frowned from me to Autumn. "What the hell are you two doing inside my closet?"

I turned sideways to hide the evidence on my pants.

"We came for a bucket to clean up a spill," Autumn said shrilly. "Nothing else. We . . . haven't done anything else here."

Autumn *did* want to hide it. My heart pinched, but I overrode the feeling. If she saw this as a momentary thing, I would find a way to accept it.

"The door locked, and we couldn't get out," I said smoothly. "We worried we'd be trapped here all weekend."

"I don't usually come in on a Friday night," Maryanne said. "But I wanted to get ahead of the mess in the gym before Monday."

"We'll get out of your way, then." I urged Autumn out of the small room ahead of me. "Thank you."

Maryanne nodded, her long gray ponytail swaying across the back of her blue uniform. "I can't imagine how the door locked." She followed us into the locker room.

"Me either," Autumn said, her gaze trained on the floor.

She appeared embarrassed about what we did. Maybe she wasn't attracted to me, which was irritating. I'd liked her almost from the moment I met her, and I'd tried to send signals that I was interested. As an orc would do with a potential mate, I'd smiled at her when I saw her. I'd given her my seat on the bleachers at the pep rally two weeks ago. And I'd brought her favorite cookies to the teachers' lounge one morning and watched to make sure she saw them.

Wait. I hadn't taken advantage of her just now, had I?

As we left the locker room, crossed the open gym floor that definitely needed cleaning, and exited out into the main hallway, we said nothing.

I smacked my forehead with my palm, and she shot me a confused look.

I *had* taken advantage of her. The mating signals I'd deployed? They hadn't worked because I'd forgotten everything else. If a female didn't indicate return interest, the male must back away and leave her alone. She was allowed to choose who she mated with.

We went to the teachers' lounge, and she opened the cabinet holding her personal possessions, removing a bag she slung over her shoulder.

Turning, she frowned my way. "I . . ." She shook her head. "I'll see you Monday morning?"

The monthly staff meeting would take place in the conference room. This was when the administrative team discussed ongoing projects or any changes in how lesson plans must be enacted.

"Yes." My voice came out dull, but I was disappointed. I'd hoped after what happened she'd indicate she wanted to be with me. "I'll walk with you to your car."

"Thanks."

She led the way, and I followed, trying not to admire her lush shape as she strode from the building and across the nearly empty lot.

Silly me. I'd even parked my vehicle next to hers, hoping to walk with her after the dance. I'd hoped to speak with her, woo her.

Now we walked in silence.

After she was seated inside her small vehicle, I strode to mine and climbed inside. I didn't engage the engine. I sat like a slug, watching as she drove from the lot and out onto the road.

I remained where I was long past the time her vehicle's back lights had disappeared into the night. My dreams of a possible life with Autumn disappeared along with her.

Perhaps it was for the best. I was huge compared to her. I'd felt her tight passage constricting around my fingers. Even with four fingers inside her, the stretch wasn't what she'd receive from my cock.

Our full mating could hurt her.

CHAPTER 7
AUTUMN

When the janitor walked in, nearly catching me mid-orgasm, it felt as if a switch had been flicked, reverting me back to the shy woman who hadn't dared say more than a peep to Thraal.

As we walked to the teachers' lounge, grabbed our things, then strode to the parking lot, I kept hoping he'd mention what happened. Maybe suggest we get together sometime after work.

Instead, he remained as quiet as me.

Was he already regretting what had happened? He must be. Otherwise, he'd bring it up, right?

I'd done research into orc mating rituals online, though there wasn't much. Basically, if an orc was interested, he'd state his intentions clearly. If the woman indicated interest, he'd claim her. If the couple was sexually compatible, they'd pursue a full mating with an orc-ish house, a backyard, and three point two mini orcs scampering around.

Thraal hadn't done that, and I'd hung around to give him a chance to pursue me if he chose.

Dejected, I drove home, struggling not to cry.

My warm rush of satisfaction faded, replaced by sadness. I needed to continue with my life, not hang around waiting for him to notice me.

I could try out that new dating service I'd found online. See if someone else could spark my interest.

"I doubt it," I whispered. My initial admiration for Thraal had slowly evolved into caring. And after he showed me so much pleasure in the closet, I'd begun to fall in love.

"Yeah, and see where that got you," I hissed into the rearview mirror.

When I reached my apartment building, I parked and went inside.

It was late. I needed to sleep on this before making any decisions. In fact, I had the entire weekend to figure out if this meant anything.

I climbed into bed and my kitty, Miso, leapt up and stretched out beside me.

"At least you want to sleep with me," I whispered.

He purred and tried to snag my hand with his claws.

"Yeah, love you too."

Thankfully, I fell asleep not long after that.

MONDAY MORNING, I was late leaving my apartment for work. It was Miso's fault. He loved getting on the counter and knocking things off. In this morning's case, my freshly poured cup of coffee. Having it splatter all over my tiny kitchen wasn't bad enough. Nope. It also splattered on me.

The mid-thigh skirt I'd snatched out of the closet swished as I hurried across the parking lot and into the school building. I rushed down the empty hall and into the conference room.

Kassia waved as I scooted around the table, passing sitting orcs and humans. The principal cleared her throat and lifted her brows, glancing at the clock on the wall. Yeah, two minutes late. Sue me.

I dropped into the seat beside my friend, noting Thraal sitting directly across from me.

His gaze met mine, and his scowl matched that of the principal before he opened a notebook on the table.

"Catch up later?" Kassia asked softly by my ear. "You didn't reply to my texts all weekend."

Because I didn't want to get into what happened in the janitor's closet. I'd taken long walks that didn't give me any resolution, then stared at the TV while three entire seasons of Girl in Flames flashed across the screen.

Even playing with Miso didn't cheer me up.

The principal cleared her throat. "If you'll review the new proposed budget I've passed around, we can discuss how we're going to make up the shortfalls."

Ugh. The community wanted their kids to have the best education possible, something me and my fellow teachers scrambled to make happen. But taxpayers were never eager to give us what we needed to ensure we could deliver it.

Grumbles rang out in the room.

"As you'll note, our arts and music departments have taken a sizeable hit," the principal said.

Our creative art teacher sniffed. The orc music teacher snarled.

"As you'll also note," the principal said. "One of the few departments that didn't suffer is the sport's department."

Was anyone surprised? Nothing against the football and soccer teams, but art and music expanded the mind.

"I'm not going to stand for it," the principal said, her

voice rising to a screech. "I'm shifting funds from sports over to arts and music."

"Are you allowed to do that?" the vice principal asked, shifting in his chair.

"Who knows?" she said. "I'm doing it. However . . ." She held up a finger when the room erupted with conversation, "I'm not opposed to ensuring sports is fully funded."

That quieted everyone down.

"I've come up with some fundraising tasks for all of you that will make sure each team has what they need. If you'll flip the budget paper over, you'll see your assignment."

Kassie and I shared a raised eyebrow look before turning over our papers. Because she gasped; I looked at hers first. She and Jarum had been paired and tasked with fundraising new nets for the soccer team.

Her grin widened when she took in my paper.

Thraal and Autumn will fundraise for new varsity field hockey uniforms.

CHAPTER 8

THRAAL

I couldn't work with Autumn. Even sitting across from her brought on inappropriate thoughts.

I'd noted her short skirt when she rushed into the room, and when she removed her cardigan and sat, her button-up shirt shifted in the front, hinting at the swell of her breasts.

I was an orc creep and the sooner I acknowledged it, the better. Were there orc support groups for things like that?

As the principal wrapped up the meeting, my gaze met Autumn's. I couldn't read her expression. What did she think about us working together to fundraise?

"Please take the next twenty minutes to get together with your teammate and come up with a strategy," the principal said. "But don't be late for your first class!"

Twenty minutes, huh?

More grumbles rang out in the room. Teachers took on huge workloads already. Who'd have time to squeeze in fundraising?

My friend, Jarum, sat beside me, staring at Kassia. He'd confided to me that he liked her, though he hadn't acted on his interest. From the eagerness in her eyes when she looked at him, I suspected she felt the same.

My chest tightened with envy. I wished him the best. It was too bad the best wasn't in store for me.

I scraped back my chair, meeting Autumn's gaze. "Where would you like to discuss this?"

She shrugged. "Anywhere."

Groups filed out of the conference room. Since Kassia had joined Jarum, sitting beside him here, I opted to find a different place to talk.

Autumn followed me out into the hall. "It looks like the teachers' lounge is taken," she said, waving to where four of our fellow teachers were entering the room next to the conference room.

"How about a classroom?" I said.

"If you think we can come up with a solution fast. Some students like to get to class early."

"How about . . ." I frowned, thinking. "The gym?"

"Sure."

We walked down the hall and entered the big open room. Finding no one else inside, I climbed a few levels up the bleachers and sat.

Autumn followed but stared down at me for a moment before climbing five more levels up and dropping onto the flat wooden surface near the edge.

"Don't fall," I said, peering at the gap between the two sets of bleachers.

"I won't." She lowered her tote bag beside her feet and tugged out a pad of paper and a pen. "Where should we start?"

With a huff, I climbed the bleachers and sat on the same level, keeping an orc's length between us.

"We can consider the standard fundraising techniques,"

she said with a roll of her eyes. "Bake sales, car washes, and split raffles."

"What do field hockey uniforms cost?" I asked, having no idea. I'd seen people playing the sport after classes ended for the day, but I'd never remained to watch a game.

"Let me see." Frowning, she scrolled into her phone. "Custom for each team player is out. Unless we want to fundraise each year, it would be best to keep them generic. Just a number."

"We need the school name and colors," I said with a grunt.

She leveled me a look I couldn't define. "That seems to be standard. Eleven players including the goalie, who'll need a complete uniform as well. There'll be more than eleven players, however, some sitting on the bench, rotating in and out of play."

"We can ask the coach for a solid number."

She nodded. "My assumption is that the JV team will use the Varsity uniforms now. That seems to be the norm." She frowned at her phone. "Sleeveless or not?"

"What would they prefer?"

"No idea. But the price for either is between seventy-five and a hundred dollars per player, and that's without the goalie. Goalie equipment can run in the thousands of dollars."

I sucked in a breath and released it. "A loose number for, say, twenty players plus two goalies is seven to eight thousand dollars. We'll have to sell a lot of cookies to come up with that."

"It was just a suggestion," she said softly.

"I'm not criticizing."

"It sounded like it."

"I'm grumbly, okay?" I snapped.

"Yeah, right." she whispered.

"I heard that."

"I'm sure you did." She dropped her pen onto her paper and sent me another look I couldn't define. "What ideas do *you* have for raising money?"

"Well, I think—"

Her pen rolled off her pad of paper. It plunked on the edge of the bleacher bench and tumbled over the side, falling between the two sets of bleachers.

For a reason beyond my comprehension, Autumn leaned over as if she thought she could grab it.

When she yelped and started falling, I leapt toward her.

CHAPTER 9
AUTUMN

I braced myself for impact.

I did not brace myself for Thraal to play Superman. He latched onto my ankle. Unsettled, he tumbled into the gap behind me.

We fell between the bleachers, smacking onto the floor. *He* smacked onto the floor, that is. I landed on top of him, straddling his thighs.

Holding his shoulders, I lifted my upper body, though I couldn't rise far without hitting my head on the bleachers above us.

Being this close to him reminded me of what we'd done in the janitor's closet and how he'd rejected me after, like it was convenient to kiss me and finger fuck me because we were trapped, but I wasn't worth another thought after that.

Something poked me between the legs.

Oh, jeez.

"Why do you have a hard-on?" I snarled.

"I don't," he snapped.

"Let me guess. That's just a test tube in your pants?" I

wiggled against him but stopped when I realized I was getting as turned on by our closeness as him.

"I'm much bigger than a test tube," he said, one corner of his lips curling up. Straightening his glasses, he leveled me a look I couldn't understand. If I didn't know better, I'd think he was flirting.

He had no right to look this sexy.

"Okay, then," I said. "It's a flashlight."

His full smile made my breath catch. "I'm bigger than a flashlight, too."

"That's not possible," I said.

"You don't teach biology. If you did, you'd know it's entirely possible."

"I don't believe you."

"I'm more than happy to prove it." He undid the top button of his pants.

My breathing picked up, and my pulse rocketed through the top of my head. I leaned into him, arching my spine and shifting my hips, rubbing against him.

Until I realized what I was doing.

Why was I straddling him? I should be climbing out of here by now. I definitely shouldn't be giving into his lure.

"You don't have a hard-on because you don't want me," I said.

"What makes you think that?" A tic bloomed in his temple, thumping quickly as if his heart was leaping around in his chest as much as mine.

"You rejected me."

"My fingers did no such thing." He shifted us around until I lay beneath him.

Gulping, I swallowed, but the lump in my throat wouldn't go down.

"Your fingers meant nothing," I said, lifting my chin.

My feelings were still hurt from him remaining silent after we got out of the closet. I'd hung around my apartment Saturday and Sunday, keeping my phone handy because I'd expected to hear something from him. Maybe not an invitation for a date, but even an *I'll call you sometime* would've been nice.

"Is that what you think?" he growled, placing his palm on my bare thigh. He watched me as his hand started creating circles, moving higher with each one. "I dare you to tell me to stop." His hand crept closer to where I needed him, and he groaned when his thumb touched between my legs. "Why are you wet?"

"Well, I didn't pee myself."

"You say my fingers meant nothing, that what we did the other night meant nothing, but I suspect you want this." A twist of his hand, and he'd shoved my panties to the side. His finger dipped between my folds. "Don't you?"

I couldn't think, and he wanted me to respond to a question?

Moaning, I jerked my hips up toward his hand. "I hate that I want you."

A frown creased his knobby forehead. "Why do you hate that I can give you pleasure?"

"Because you don't want me. I'm a convenient body to . . . Okay, to pleasure."

"Do you truly believe I'd do this with anyone?" He tilted his head as if he couldn't fathom how such a thought could occur to me.

I had to hand it to him. Even during a somewhat civilized conversation, one part of his brain maintained focus on his fingers buried in my pussy. They kept stroking me, driving me higher.

"If you did, you would've called," I said.

"I don't have your number."

"Did you consider asking?" Hold on. "Wait. Would you have called me if you had my number?"

His fingers paused, and frankly, my clit was protesting big time. When I shifted my hips, he started stroking me again. "I—"

"Hey, what are you kids doing underneath the bleachers?" Maryanne called out. "Get out of there now, or I'm coming in to collect you and then I'm phoning your parents."

"Shit, the janitor," I hissed.

Thraal's hand jerked away from my groin, and he hurtled himself off me, smacking the back of his head on the underside of the bleachers.

The janitor slammed her palm on a seat. "Out of there. Now!"

"Allow me to handle this?" Thraal whispered.

I nodded, my face getting hotter than the time I'd spent a day hiking without wearing sunscreen.

He secured his clothing quickly while I did the same. He latched onto the bleachers above and lifted himself out easily. I gaped, envying his physical abilities.

"Thraal?" Maryanne barked.

Realizing I'd have to crawl toward the front to extricate myself from the trap, I dropped to my hands and knees.

"Here," he said, extending his arm my way. "I'll help."

I took it, and he pulled me up to stand beside him with ease.

"You're strong," I said, my face getting hot.

"I'm an orc," he said proudly.

"And Autumn." Maryanne huffed. "I should've guessed. What were you two doing beneath the bleachers?" She stomped over to stand on the gym floor below us. "This is the second time I've caught you two in a place where you don't belong. If you keep this up, I'm going to have to report you."

"I fell," I said. "Thraal grabbed my ankle but was tugged down along with me. Truly, there shouldn't be a gap between the bleachers. Someone could get hurt."

Thraal grunted helpfully.

"Oh, my, you're right." Maryanne's eyes widened, and she pressed her palm against her chest. "Are you okay?"

"Yes, we're fine. I'm not injured at all," I said. "How about you Thraal?"

"Not even a bruise."

"Well, you'd better let the school nurse check you out just in case," Maryanne said. "Liability and all that."

"Sure." I wanted to burst into laughter, though it might come out high-pitched.

Something had changed between me and Thraal.

Would it hold?

Or would he go cold the second we walked from the room?

CHAPTER 10

THRAAL

Something was different between us.

I suspected Autumn *liked* me.

What could I do about it? First, I wouldn't ignore her. I'd assumed she wasn't interested and didn't want to pressure her for something she wasn't prepared to give.

Tonight, I'd study human mating practices and deploy them with Autumn.

"I'll fix the bleachers," Maryanne said, striding down to the end, where she started pushing. The enormous wood and metal structure didn't move an inch.

I walked over to her and added my strength to her endeavors, and the bleachers smacked together.

"Amazing." She looked me up and down. "Do you work out?"

I shrugged. "I'm an orc. We're very strong."

"Hmm," she said. "I've been trying to convince the school to hire more janitorial staff. I'll recommend orcs."

"That's very kind of you." I hurried back to where Autumn waited, a bemused expression on her face.

"Don't forget to get checked out by the school nurse," Maryanne called out as we left the gym.

"Should we go to the nurse's office?" I asked softly as we walked out into the hall.

"I'm fine," Autumn said, giving me a smile that I had to admit was beautiful despite her lack of tusks. "Do you feel okay?"

"I don't wish to see the nurse."

"Then let's skip it." She paused in the hall and laid her hand on my arm. The muscle flexed from her touch. "That was sweet of you to help Maryanne."

"I'm strong." It was common for an orc to use his strength to impress a potential mate. I watched her face, enjoying the pretty color that kept blooming there. Orcs were green. While our skin might grow heated if we were embarrassed, it did not change color like Autumn's.

I liked this. It gave me a hint into her feelings. What other clues would she reveal? I'd watch and see.

"Were you impressed with my strength?" I asked.

"I was." With a grin, she leaned against my arm as we started walking again, almost as if we were a couple. It stunned me, and I tripped over nothing, catching myself but feeling heat in my face.

"Watch out. That tile jumped right up at you," she said, her grin widening.

She wasn't embarrassed to be seen with an orc who'd done something foolish? This was worth thinking about.

"We have a few minutes left before classes," I said. "That's probably not enough time to come up with ideas for raising funds. Are you available to meet after school?"

"Not today. I've got plans. Sorry. Tomorrow?"

"We could meet before classes or after they let out.

Whichever is best for you." I shouldn't be disappointed. I wanted to see her all the time.

"Either works for me."

"After school, it is. Then, if we need more time, we won't feel pressured to get to class."

"Perfect." She stopped outside her classroom. "Thank you for rescuing me from under the bleachers and keeping me from crashing on the floor."

I dipped forward in a short bow, an orc sign of respect. "Anytime."

She turned the doorknob. "Let's hope I don't fall again, but if I do, I hope it's with you."

My face grew hotter. She did like me!

Her fingertips stroked down my cheek, though she had to hop up to reach. "So cute. Too cute, I think." With a wink, she turned and entered the classroom.

I'd tripped, and she hadn't chided me.

I'd blushed, and she'd liked it.

I strode toward my first class, stunned at the thought that she could see a male showing such behavior in a favorable light. Orc females would despise a male who did anything like that.

It appeared my mating strategy needed a realignment.

CHAPTER 11
AUTUMN

"And then he latched onto my leg and fell down between the bleachers with me, twisting so I landed on top of him," I said to Kassia. We sat on my tiny back deck overlooking my apartment building's parking lot.

Miso had flopped on the wooden decking under my chair, and every time I moved, he reached out and tried to snag my leg with his claws, his version of affection.

I dangled a piece of string with a toy on the end to distract him and he grabbed onto it, wrangling it with his back legs kicking.

"You fell on top of Thraal, huh?" Kassia asked, her pretty green eyes sparkling. She twisted a strand of her long blonde hair around her finger. "What happened after that?"

I usually shared everything with Kassia, but for some reason, I hesitated now. "He's really sweet. Did I tell you that he helped Maryanne move the bleachers so no one else would fall between them?"

"You did not, and I agree that's sweet, but you also did not tell me what you two did while you lounged underneath the bleachers." She shook her finger at me. Lifting her glass of wine from the small table between our two chairs, she took a sip. "Anything exciting you need to share?"

I sighed. "All I'm going to say is that it's fun kissing a guy with tusks."

"Whoa. Kissing. Ha." Her head tilted.

"Would you want to be caught making out or doing something more with a guy beneath the bleachers?" I swirled my wine around in my glass and kicked my feet up on the wooden rail surrounding the tiny deck. It wasn't much for outdoor space, and my rent was fifty more a month than those without a deck, but it was worth every penny.

"If it was Jarum, I'd be awfully tempted to do more," she said.

"And so was I. How are things going between you two? Last I saw, you were crossing the conference room, aiming in his direction."

"They're going . . . very well." Color filled her face.

"What?" I gasped. "Why didn't you tell me?"

"Probably for the same reason you haven't shared much about Thraal. It's so new and wonderful and special, and I guess I didn't want to jinx it by bringing it up."

"Are you two . . ." I twirled my fingers around.

"Not all the way, though I bet it won't be long."

"Yay!" I leapt up and gave her a hug. "I'm so happy for you two."

"Well, we're only dating so far, so don't get too excited."

"Still."

"Still," she said with a grin. "Can you believe the principal roped us into fundraising? Soccer nets are expensive."

We compared prices and exchanged ideas, but neither of us had much to offer that we hadn't already discussed with our partners.

"How are you and Thraal going to raise the money you need?" she asked.

"We're meeting together tomorrow after work to discuss it."

"Beneath the bleachers?" she asked with a chuckle.

I shook my head. "As tempting as that is, I don't want to get caught—again—by Maryanne."

"Sounds like Thraal's in her good graces after heroically eliminating the bleacher gap."

"We're skating on thin ice." I'd already shared some of what happened inside the janitor's closet.

She shrugged. "I doubt she cares. Maybe she's done her own hot things inside the closet."

"Maybe." I frowned. "I wonder if the field hockey shed has any old equipment we could sell. People might pay a lot for retro stuff."

"That's a fantastic idea. It won't work for the soccer nets, but I'll bring it up to Jarum." She winced. "It'll take forever to raise enough money with yard sales."

"We need fundraisers that bring in lots of money all at once. I hope Thraal has some good ideas."

"Let's also hope he has some ideas related to you, too, hon."

I lifted my wine glass her way. "I'll drink to that."

We clinked them together and took sips.

THE NEXT DAY, I waited outside Thraal's classroom while he finished. I had a free period at the end of the day and had spent the time grading the latest test I'd given.

I'd dressed in a cute skirt and top but wondered what Thraal thought of clothing that showed so much leg. Orc women tended to dress conservatively in long gowns and some even wore scarves over their hair, though that was mostly the older orcs I'd seen around town.

"There you are," Thraal said, stepping out of his classroom after the last student had left. "Where would you like to talk?"

"I was thinking we could go to the field hockey shed to see if there's anything there we could sell. We could come back here after if that works for you. The conference room should be free."

He nodded, and we left the building. The shed had been placed beneath the trees in a grassy area beyond the field hockey field. Shouts and laughter from kids getting on busses or hanging out in front of the school faded as we crossed the big open area.

"What would you think if I picked you up, flung you over my shoulder, and ran into the woods with you?" Thraal asked.

I froze, my eyes widening. My heart flipped over and sprang against my ribcage, eager. "I guess it would depend on what you wanted to do in the woods."

"Are you saying no?"

I gulped. "I should mention my ex."

"Why?"

"He was controlling. Demanding. I don't know if I'm up for something like that."

"I see."

We stopped in front of the shed, and I undid the padlock, using the combination I'd obtained from the front office. It dropped from my limp fingers as I creaked open the wooden door.

I stepped inside the shed and paused to let my eyes

adjust to the darkness. The inside was about ten by ten and full of all kinds of rubble.

He followed, and the door swung shut behind him, leaving us in darkness heavy with the weight of unspoken emotions.

Was he offering what I thought he was? He had to name it, though. I didn't want to misunderstand his intentions.

"I want to claim you," he said in a deep, gravelly voice.

Aw, hell. I kind of wanted to be claimed, too, but what if letting him do more turned him into my ex?

However, Thraal wasn't anything like my ex. I needed to remember that.

"Why don't you test it out and see what happens?" I croaked, my throat closing off with anticipation. This was it! We were going to . . . I wasn't sure what, but it might involve kissing and maybe even some finger action, something I'd welcome.

He lifted me up and pressed me back against the shed wall. "What about this?" His mouth crashed down on mine.

I lost all control, clinging to his shoulders as his mouth plundered. His tongue staked a claim on mine while his fingers roamed down my sides. One hand glided down to cup one of my ass cheeks, and when he squeezed, a moan ripped up my throat.

I teased my fingers through his thick hair, tugging away the strand of leather he used to pin it back. His horns called to me, and I traced my fingertips down them.

He groaned, his head lifting. He studied me in the dim light.

"In the woods, I'd also do this." He tugged up my shirt and cupped one of my breasts, his thumb stroking the nipple through the fabric. My nipple perked up, shouting it liked what he was doing. "Is this acceptable?"

"Yes."

"You're aroused. I can smell it."

Should a girl be embarrassed by something like that?

Nah.

"What are you going to do about my arousal?" I asked, and even I could hear the sauciness in my voice.

"I'll make you so aroused you scream out my name when you come."

"I believe you're going to have to show me exactly what you mean, Thraal."

With a growl, he sliced through my underwear with a claw. He retracted his claws and plunged the finger inside me. Watching my face, he undid the front of his pants. "You're wet. Let me see if I can make you wetter before you find your pleasure."

CHAPTER 12
THRAAL

We weren't in the woods, but I was going to claim her as mine. What might happen after that, I didn't know, but I would seduce her in the orc way, and we'd talk about where we were going after that.

I drove my thumb inside her, nearly coming from how amazing her sweet little passage felt contracting around my digit.

"I'm big," I said, though we'd already discussed that.

"Show me," she said, rocking against my hand.

"Do you mean that?"

She bobbed her head, her pupils blown. "I do."

I wrenched my pants down and kicked them aside. My cock slammed against my abs; a long, thick, knobby thing as rough as me.

"See me," I said. "Then tell me if you don't want more." In orc tradition, I wouldn't have to obtain consent at a time like this. She'd already indicated interest. When a male took a female to the woods, what happened next was well understood. If she didn't wish to mate, she'd make it clear, usually by stabbing a blade in his back after he flung her over his shoulder. It wouldn't cause him true harm, but it would make it clear she wasn't available for claiming.

Autumn had no knife, and I hadn't carried her into the woods, so the rules had to be bent before I could be with her fully.

"I want more," she groaned, shifting her hips forward to take all of my thumb.

My body tensed. "Everything?"

"Yes."

Ahhh. "Then you shall have it, mate."

I continued to rub her clit, savoring her sighs of pleasure and the way her passage tightened around my thumb.

When I pulled it out, the heady scent of her arousal nearly consumed me. My cock was on fire, eager to plunder deep within her.

Her legs tightened around my hips. "No," she cried. "Keep it there."

"I'm going to take you hard against the wall," I said. "Yes?"

"Yes," she breathed against my chest.

I placed the head of my cock at her entrance. Then I tilted her head up so she'd meet my eyes.

A jerk of my hips, and I pushed myself inside her.

CHAPTER 13

AUTUMN

All my dreams were coming true, and they centered around Thraal's knobby cock seated within me. Man, he was huge. I could barely take him all, and he was so wide, it stung when he shoved everything he had inside me.

"Are you with me?" he growled, pausing. His cock throbbed, and something on the sides hummed. Did the lumps I'd seen in the dim light vibrate? Hallelujah.

"Yes." I kept my eyes on his. We couldn't kiss. I was so much shorter than him, my mouth only reached the line of his nipples. I sucked one into my mouth and ran my tongue across it.

Groaning, he pulled out and rocked his hips forward, burying his cock inside me again.

I gasped as the bent end of his cock pressed down hard on my G-spot as it passed. It hit just right, as did something above his cock that glided through my wetness and across my clit.

"Shit, I'm going to come," I said.

"Scream when you do it. I want to hear your cries echoing around us." He picked up his pace, slamming into me, the spur above his cock rubbing my clit until it throbbed with anticipation.

My body trembled and my heart raced. Tall and muscular, he easily supported my weight. His sharp eyes pierced my own, the intensity of his gaze driving my heat higher. I reached up and tugged on his hair.

His thrusts were deep and intense, pushing me closer and closer to the edge. He kept one hand under my butt, steadying me as he brought me deeper into pleasure.

Tension gathered in my body as I moved with him, rocking my hips up to take everything he could offer. Every thrust brought me closer to an orgasm, and I moaned over and over, my body shaking. As his body tightened, he went faster, driving me along with him. I pressed my forehead against his chest and sucked in the wonderful feelings he generated inside me.

Bliss washed over me, and I shouted his name, my body shuddering with the intensity of my orgasm.

Slowing his pace, he watched me ride each crest, my body succumbing to something I'd never felt before. I'd had sex. I'd had orgasms. But nothing in my past compared to this.

He pulled out of me, his cock still harder than a pole, glistening with my wetness. Precum coated the tip, a thick, green cream I wanted to taste.

After lowering me to my feet, he tugged me over to a pile of mats stacked on the floor, bending me forward on my belly and hefting me up until my body aligned with his.

"I need to hear you scream some more, mate," he growled, pushing into me again.

I was spiraling already, still riding the last orgasm while the next one shouted it would be more than happy to rock through paradise again.

He started pumping inside me, pushing hard, the motion jerking me and the pile of mats.

His fingers found my clit, and he rolled it while moving faster, pushing me so high, my head was among the clouds.

In no time, I was hurtling toward the abyss.

My orgasm shot through me, and I groaned.

He leaned over me, pushing deep inside me. "Scream, Autumn. Give it to me, mate. It's mine, and I'm claiming it just as I'm claiming you."

I gave way, giving him everything he asked for and more.

CHAPTER 14

THRAAL

My mate was amazing, so lush and responsive. I'd crave her for the rest of my days.

As her body quivered, her passage sucked on my cock. I couldn't hold back. With a hoarse cry, I pumped faster, riding her pleasure until I gave into my own with a crash.

My seed shot within her, thick spurts that coated her inner walls.

I braced myself over her, our bodies still connected, feeling the head of my cock swell.

"You're getting bigger," she said, her voice muffled by the rubber mats.

"I'm knotting."

"Why didn't I know that about orcs?"

"You haven't fucked one?"

Her body shook with her laugh. "It seems I'm getting a quick education by our school's geeky chemistry teacher."

Since we'd remain locked together for some time, I lifted her enough to remove a few mats from the pile, tossing them onto the wooden floor. Dropping down onto the lower group, I took her with me, spooning her while my cock continued to expand inside her.

"What is greeky?" I asked.

"A geek is someone of high intellect who's very knowledgeable about a subject."

"If I'm greeky, then so are you. You impress me with your understanding of mathematics."

"I believe you've shown me a new form of chemical reaction. I'm surprised every woman, plus a bunch of guys, haven't mated with orcs."

"Eh, some are frightened by our size or the color of our skin. Humans appear to prefer smooth foreheads without the knobby structures so common among orcs. Perhaps they don't like bulging muscles?"

"Then they're out of their minds." She stroked my arm wrapped around her.

"You'll move in with me this weekend."

She froze. "What do you mean?"

"We're mated. It's only proper that we live together."

"Are you proposing to me?"

If only I could see her face. I couldn't read her feelings from her tone of voice. "I don't need to. You're already mine."

She scrambled away from me, stretching my cock until it dragged out of her, the thick end making a pop when her body released it.

"You're supposed to wait for the knot to go down," I said. "How else will my seed remain inside you to give you a child?"

Rising to her feet, she stared down at me. "Child? Move in with you?!"

I let my gaze travel down her gorgeous form. "You'll be a good mate for me. I like how you responded to my cock."

Her hands smacked on her hips. "Hold it right there. You think because we just had sex that we're now married?"

Frowning, I got to my feet. "That's correct."

"No proposal. No wooing me." Her voice rose to a screech. "Just hey, we had sex, so now you're having my babies?"

"That is how it's done among orcs."

She raked her hair off her face. During our mating, it had come out of the snug arrangement she'd made on the top of her head. "That's not how it's done among humans."

"It's in the treaty."

"I haven't read the treaty."

"Why not? If you wish to be intimate with us, you should understand our mating customs."

She started pacing, pausing to growl and look down at my seed oozing down her thighs. "How much of this stuff did you pump inside me? A gallon?"

"Not quite. Perhaps a cup. I've never measured it."

"Most guys would," she huffed. She stormed up to me and poked my chest, a puny gesture that I barely felt. "We're *not* married."

"Mated."

"We're not mated either."

It was all I could do to take my eyes off her jiggling breasts. I needed to lick them, suck on the big nipples as soon as possible. Fill her with more of my cum. "We are. You'll move in with me this weekend."

"Not until you woo me properly."

I frowned. "I don't recall seeing that in the treaty."

"Call it the Thraal-Autumn Treaty."

"I don't believe such a thing exists."

"We just signed it."

"Ah." I suddenly realized what she was saying. "You don't feel I've shown you enough pleasure yet. That does occur among orcs." I tugged her against me. "Allow me to suck on your clit. Then I'll pump more cum inside you and you'll be happy with our new arrangement."

"I can't believe you think I only need good sex to become yours."

"Excellent sex."

She rolled her eyes. "Whatever."

I tilted my head. "Isn't that enough among humans?"

She sighed. "Maybe a woman would like some hearts and flowers stuff every now and then before she suddenly belongs to someone."

"Then this shall be yours," I said, pressing my fist against my chest to solidify my vow. My cock started rising, eager once more. "We'll begin the heart and flower stuff soon, but for now, I will suck on your clit."

CHAPTER 15
AUTUMN

I should be leaping for joy. Thraal wanted me.

But he thought we were married, and just because we'd had amazing sex and his cum was leaking down my legs didn't mean I was his possession.

"Here's the thing," I said. "My ex told me what to do and when to do it, and when I ended it, I told myself I'd never let another guy do that to me ever again."

Thraal dipped his head forward in a bow. "I apologize for ever giving you the impression I would demand and expect you to act. I realize I've circumvented the protocols, but I'll ensure they're completed as is needed." His brow scrunched together. "Would sucking on your clit help to compensate for my oversight?"

Swoon.

"It might," I said, tapping my chin. Jeez, how could I be mad when he was so cute about this?

With a grin, Thraal scooped me up and laid me down on the pile of mats. "Allow me to make this up to you."

Who was I to complain when a guy wanted to make things right between us by sucking on my clit?

He crawled up over me and kissed me, and I soon lost track of where we were, what we'd been talking about, and if the world was flat or round.

He trailed his tusks across my jawline and down my neck, gently biting my skin. Sucking one of my nipples into his mouth, he nibbled on it with his tusks while I groaned and writhed beneath him.

His fingers dipped through the wet folds between my legs, and he released my nipple with a pop, grinning up at me. "I like that you're dripping with my cum. I'm going to fill you up again soon."

I shouldn't be excited about him dumping another cup full inside me, but I strangely was.

He kissed across my chest and then stooped between my legs, hitching them up over his shoulders.

"Spread yourself for me, mate," he growled.

Growling could be good when it was delivered by Thraal. It must be about perspective. I was hot for him, so the sound tickled across my bones.

He leaned in close and licked me. Did he like the taste of his cum mixed in with my juices? He must because he plunged his tongue inside me, showing me how long and thick it was. Not as big as his cock, but it was a huge cock. I still couldn't believe it fit inside me.

Sliding his tongue out of my passage, he ran it across my clit, then drove it into my passage again. Over and over, while my eyes rolled back in my head, and I released endless cries. They echoed in the small space, and I was grateful there wasn't a field hockey game today. They'd think wild animals were trapped inside the shed.

He drew his tongue out of me and sucked my clit into his mouth. He laved it, rubbing his scratchy tongue over it while I bucked up toward him and panted.

Rising up over me, he snarled. "I'm going to fuck you hard again, mate. Prepare yourself."

He was going alpha again, but I couldn't find the brain-power to tell him to behave.

As he flipped me over and spread my legs wide, I decided I'd talk to him about boundaries once he'd finished.

CHAPTER 16

THRAAL

My mate was tight, hot, and incredibly wet. I couldn't get enough of her.

I hefted her hips and placed the thick head of my cock at her opening. She dripped for me, and there wasn't anything more exciting for an orc than that.

Later, I'd need to think about how I'd deliver what she needed before she was willing to be my full mate. For now, it was important that I make her come.

I shifted my hips forward, burying my length inside her, and she groaned into the mat.

Because it was important that she come before me, I reached underneath and rolled her clit, rocking against her while she pushed back to meet me.

"Good mate," I growled. "Like that." I knew she didn't want me trying to control her, but I was an orc. Acting like this was in my nature. I'd temper my behavior, however, because I wanted to please her. My heart would be crushed if she turned me away.

Soon, I lost all thought of ways I could woo her and

focused solely on the feel of my cock thickening, my balls bunching up, and her soft cries of pleasure.

I tugged on her clit, loving how it swelled with her passion and how her tight little body accepted everything I had to offer.

It was hard to believe I'd thought we wouldn't fit.

My pulse soared. I still couldn't believe I was mating with Autumn, that she wanted me. I'd do everything within my power to make sure she wanted me for the rest of our days.

When she gasped, and her passage started sucking and jerking on my cock, I plunged into her faster, pulling out and driving her across the peak and down the other side. She continued to shudder and cry out as I pumped into her.

When she sagged, her body spent, I filled her with more cum.

I HELD her on my chest while reclining on the cushions until my knot finally receded.

Then I tapped her ass. "We need to do what we came here for."

"It seems you already did."

I rose to look down at her. "Do you think I lured you here solely to fill you with my cum?"

"From the wetness between my legs, it sure feels like it." The lazy satisfaction in her voice made my heart flounder. It would be very easy to love my mate, as I should. But she still needed hearts and flowers. What if I didn't do this right?

Despite my worry, my chest puffed. I may be what she'd

call a greek—no, *geek*—but I was a geek who could make sure his mate was well pleasured.

"We were going to see if there was anything we could sell to raise money for the uniforms," I said.

Perhaps the best way to handle that would be with a donation. When orcs emerged from the hills, many of us brought stones and precious metals we'd mined below the ground. Humans gushed and offered us vehicles and even homes as long as we were willing to part with some of our underground wealth. It hadn't taken the original orc settlers long to realize we could be taken advantage of.

My older brother, Vestalon, had managed what we brought, selling it carefully and placing the equivalent coins in the bank, an equal amount under each of our names. He was so good at this, he now worked for the bank.

My share would last me ten lifetimes, but what need did I have for wealth? What I sought most rested in my arms at this moment.

The point was, I could donate the money without making a slight dent in my bank account.

But doing so would mean our task was finished, and I wasn't anywhere near done with Autumn.

I tapped her ass again. "Start looking around, mate."

She scowled. "What did I say about acting controlling?"

"Please?"

Her lips twitched upward. "Are you always like this?"

"Like what?" I let my fingers roam across her delectable body. If she stayed here much longer, I was going to claim her once again. Mating her would drive my heat to a fever pitch, and once it crested, I'd need to fill her with cum multiple times a day.

For now, I'd hold my heat back. She said it was important that I woo her.

And pleasing her was the most important thing in the world to me.

CHAPTER 17

AUTUMN

We dressed and poked around inside the shed, finding some retro equipment that might fetch a decent price online. The uniforms had to be from the 1950s, and there must be some value in stuff like that. We dragged everything out of the back of the shed and placed it near the entrance.

I shoved my hair off my face. It had long since come out of the pretty arrangement I'd made this morning, but who cared? I'd been well and truly fucked, and with my bones humming, all I could think about was dragging him to the mats to do it again.

"We can take everything to the school and see where the janitor would like us to put it until we sell it," I said.

With a nod, Thraal turned the doorknob and pressed his shoulder into it.

It didn't open.

"Let me try," I said, nudging him to the side.

Still wouldn't open. This would be comical if it wasn't happening so often.

"Did you lock it when we came inside?" I asked.

"You're the one who pulled it shut."

Had I? I couldn't remember.

"Well," I said, standing back and waving my hand at the panel. "You can go all alpha on the door if you'd like."

His thick brow drew together. "Behavior like that pleases human females?"

Frankly, my clit was throbbing, and I wanted to hitch up my skirt and show him how much he was pleasing me.

I settled on a huff. "Stuff like that isn't in anyone's dating handbook, but I doubt sleeping overnight in a field hockey shed would be found there either."

"Human courtship rituals are complicated," he said grimly.

"You've got that right." Moving closer, I studied the door. "It doesn't appear very sturdy. You can He-Man your way through, and we'll apologize to the janitor and come back another time to fix it."

"Alright." He squeezed his fists together. "Stand back."

I nodded and eased over to the wall beside the door.

He rushed toward the panel like a linebacker during the Superbowl and drove his body into it.

Rebounding, he groaned and clutched his head.

I rushed toward him as he collapsed on the floor.

CHAPTER 18
THRAAL

I woke to someone stroking my brow and a low voice pleading with me to wake up.

"Autumn," I said.

Her breath caught. "You're alive."

"It will take more than a door to kill me." Although, this female just might if I couldn't convince her to be my forever mate.

Once I went into my heat, I'd need to be with her often. If not, I had no alternative but to return to our underground city and ride it out in the barred caves built for just such a process. It wouldn't be comfortable, but that was the least of my worries.

I was falling in love with my pretty little human.

I sat up and held my head when the room spun.

"You've got a concussion, I bet," she said, and it pleased me to hear concern in her voice.

"I'll be fine." Rising to my feet, I glared at the entrance. "I'll find something to break down the door."

She got to her feet. "Are you sure you're okay?"

"I am." Peering around, I spied a stack of vaulting poles in the back corner and grabbed one.

"Ah, yes," she said. "They're made of CFRP, did you know?"

"Yes, of course. And you suggest I am the greeky one here?"

"Greeky . . ." Her face cleared. "Tell you what, we're both geeky."

"Most definitely."

"Are you going to vault into the door?" she asked, backing against the wall.

"Why would I do that?"

She shrugged. "Just a thought."

"No, I'm going to do this with it." I wedged it between the door and the wall and tried to pry open the panel.

"Great idea," she said. "If it works."

"It'll work," I grated out through my teeth, straining with everything inside me.

Growling and bracing my feet, I leaned into the pole, the muscles on my arms bulging and sweat breaking out on my brow. I kept at it for a long time before pausing and releasing the pole that remained wedged in the gap.

"Giving up?" she asked.

"No," I grumbled. "I'll attack the door once again." Turning, I sat on the floor, leaning against the door. I patted my lap. "Sit."

Her eyebrows raised, and she dropped onto the mats.

"I wanted you to sit on my lap," I said.

"What if I don't want to sit on your lap?"

"You're my mate," I said. "Why wouldn't you?"

"There you go again."

I frowned. "There I go where?"

"There. Again."

"Human dating rituals are complex, but human females are even more complicated."

She pointed her fingertip my way. "Bingo."

"We are not playing a game."

"You are, and you won."

"You make no sense."

She snickered. "Because you're from Mars and I'm from Venus."

"We're both from Earth."

"Maybe." Her sigh rang out. "It means we're different."

"Our bodies found a way to fit together nicely."

"It *was* nice." She crossed her arms over her chest. I'd read this gesture indicated irritation, though I couldn't discern why she might feel this way. But I'd only been among humans for three months.

Time ticked along, and despite my trying over and over again to pry open the door, I didn't find success.

Autumn laid down on the mats and drifted to sleep. I watched over her, though I doubted we'd find many threats inside the field hockey shed.

Finally, dawn's creeping light pierced through a crack in the left wall, slicing across the room and rousing Autumn. She sat up and rubbed her face, shoving her long hair out of her eyes.

"Still here, huh?" she said with a sleepy smile that cut through my chest as easily as the sun had the side of the shed.

"Where would I go?" I asked, my voice higher pitched than I liked. I'd spend the night thinking about how I could achieve my human courtship goals as quickly as possible.

"Nowhere, I suppose." She slid off the mats and approached the door. "Would you like me to try?"

"I'm stronger than you." I rose to my feet. "Much

stronger." Grunting, I leaned into the pole, determined to make the lock break and the door pop open.

It didn't work.

"Are you sure you don't want me to try?" she asked.

With a huff, I backed away. "It's not that I doubt your strength. You're strong for one so puny."

"Thanks," she said with a thinning of her lips. Her eyes sparkled, however, and I could plunge inside them and remain within her gaze forever.

"You're welcome," I stumbled to say. I backed away from the door, gesturing to the pole. "Please feel welcome."

With a nod, she pretended to spit on both of her palms, an odd gesture, and rubbed her hands together.

"Why would spitting make a difference?" I asked, tilting my head.

"It's supposed to improve your grip."

"I see." Though I didn't. "Would some of my spit help?"

Her lips twitched, and the sparkle in her eyes deepened. "Let's see what I can do on my own first, okay?"

"Very well." I backed farther from the door.

She latched onto the pole and leaned her weight into it.

The door popped open.

CHAPTER 19

AUTUMN

"See?" I crowed, sashaying my hips and rocking my arms overhead. "See?"

"What the hell are you kids doing inside the—" Maryanne poked her head through the opening and scowled. "You two *again*?"

"We got locked inside the shed," I said.

She shook her head. "The padlock's on the ground. The door can only be locked on the outside and with the padlock." Her gaze shot from me to Thraal, and her scowl deepened. "You two have some explaining to do."

"We came to the shed yesterday afternoon to see what we could sell," I said. "We're raising funds to buy the varsity field hockey team new uniforms."

She crossed her arms over her chest and tapped her boot toe on the ground. "And it took you all night?"

"As we said, we were locked inside," Thraal said. "If you'll excuse us, we'd like to go home and rest. Classes start in a few hours."

Ugh, right. I needed to shower—forget sleep, though I'd gotten some on the mats last night.

"Don't think I won't report this," Maryanne called out to our backs as we strode across the game field.

"Please do," Thraal said. "And while you're at it, figure out how that door locked us inside." His twinkling eyes met mine. "I believe we're making a habit of this."

"It wasn't that bad. You should've joined me on the mats."

"Would you have consented to be my full mate if I had?"

"You haven't convinced me I need to mate with you yet."

"My cock did a fine job of convincing you. I filled you with my seed many times, didn't I?"

"Yeah, but it takes more than seed leaking down a girl's thighs to convince her to marry a guy."

Someone snorted behind us, and I cringed. Great. Just great.

"So that's why you two keep locking yourselves inside closets and sheds," Maryanne said as she passed us. "Why didn't you just say that? I was young once, too, you know." She stomped toward the school.

Thraal and I looked at each other and burst into laughter.

FOR THE NEXT TWO DAYS, I only saw Thraal in the high school halls, and each time I approached him, he turned and bolted in the opposite direction.

"He's changed his mind," I told Kassia. She stood beside me near the teacher's lounge, watching Thraal run away.

"I'm convinced he likes you," she said. "You two did the horizontal tango."

She'd pried most of what happened out of me last night

when we met up for our weekly dinner at Popeye's. Their biscuits were to die for.

"Then why isn't he coming near me?" I asked, my self-confidence plummeting. "He could say hi or do something." My shoulders drooped. "He said he was going to court me, and I was looking forward to seeing what he'd do."

"Maybe he's planning something big. You know, like those prom proposals."

"I doubt he's going to ask me to the prom."

She turned to face me, leaning against the wall. "Would you go with him if he asked?"

"It hardly matters since we're not in high school any longer."

"True, but there's the equivalent."

"I'm not sure I like public proposals. What if I don't want to say yes?"

Her blonde eyebrows shot up, and she twirled a strand of her long hair around her finger. "Why wouldn't you? You've been crazy about Thraal since the beginning of the school year."

"He'd have to ask nicely."

She rolled her eyes. "Please tell me you're not transferring your feelings about your controlling ex onto Thraal."

"He acted too alpha inside the shed."

Leaning close, she lowered her voice. A couple of students walked by us. "There's something to be said about a guy going alpha when he's giving you the best experience of your life."

"Maybe it wasn't the best. Maybe it was only . . . I don't know, fair."

"You said he made you come four times during just one bout on the rubber mats."

"I shared too much." But, yeah, it had been an amazing experience.

"Why don't you track him down and ask him why he's avoiding you?"

I lifted my chin. "I should."

She stared at me for a long while. "Why are you standing there, then? Go find him."

"Okay," I sighed, trudging down the hall in the direction he'd taken.

"I imagine he's in his classroom," she called out. "Go get 'em, girl. And while you're at it, make it five!"

Ha ha. Like we were going to have sex in his classroom? That was such a cliché. Teachers didn't do stuff like that in public places.

No, my inner Autumn said, they do it in janitor's closets and field hockey sheds. And under the bleachers if they can get away with it.

"Shut up," I snarled.

A pack of kids coming toward me paused and swarmed in the opposite direction like a school of fish with a shark in their midst.

"Sorry," I called out. "Just . . . practicing for a play!" Yeah, that was it.

When I reached Thraal's classroom door, I froze, unwilling to knock or peek through the slice of glass to see if he was inside.

"Just do it," I whispered to myself. "Storm in there and ask him why he's avoiding you." I pinched my eyes shut, then opened them and, before I could spin around and run away, I knocked.

Nothing happened.

I knocked again.

The door swung inward and Thraal appeared in the opening.

"Ah, there you are," he said. "I have something for you." He swung a potted plant around from behind his back and thrust it out to me. "Flowers."

I stared at a plant unlike anything I'd seen in my life.

"It has black leaves," I said brightly. "And a big black flower that . . ." When I reached out to touch it, it snarled. The flower snapped forward, gaping in the center.

Its teeth latched onto my finger.

CHAPTER 20
THRAAL

"No, no, not like that," I told Autumn, prying the sharp petals away from her hand.

She gazed at my offering in horror. "It bit me."

"It's a stelladon plant."

Backing away, she looked from the plant to me. "I've never seen anything like it before."

I nudged it toward her. "It's for you. Flowers."

As an orphan, I had no family to give her mating tests. All I could do was follow human courtship rituals until I'd convinced her to be mine. Then we could jump into orc customs to finish this off.

Her lips twitched as if she was laughing, but she couldn't be. Courtship rituals were a serious matter. "Well, it's certainly interesting. I appreciate the gift." She gingerly took it from me, holding it at arms' length. "How do I feed it? I've got a few house plants at home, but I only give them water and some fertilizer when I think of it."

"A stelladon needs to be fed more than when you think of it." Was this a mistake? Perhaps I should've given her a flower that required less care.

"What does it eat, and how do I feed it?"

My spine relaxed. She was taking this seriously, as she should. "Raw meat, of course."

"Naturally."

"Place chunks near the stelladon's pot or, if you prefer, you can use an eating utensil to poke it into the plant's mouth. Water is helpful as well, but again, don't place your hand too close to the flower or . . ."

"It'll bite?"

"It could take off your arm once it gets bigger."

She gazed down at it with wide eyes. "How big is this thing going to get?"

"The usual size."

"Which is?"

"I don't believe it'll grow taller than you."

"That's reassuring." Her eyes glowed.

I leaned close to examine them. "Why do your eyes appear to shimmer?"

"I'm . . . just happy." She smiled. "That's it. I'm happy about the flower you've given me."

"Very well," I said. "I will bring your other required courting items to your residence this evening."

"Oh, wonderful," she said brightly. "That sounds . . . wonderful. I look forward to it."

As she should.

I bowed. "I must go prepare." The next courtship task would prove more of a challenge.

"About what time can I expect you?"

"After the evening meal."

"Great. I'll look forward to it." She braced the edge of the pot on her hip, and the flower poked at her shirt, seeking flesh. As long as she kept her hands away from it, she should remain safe.

However, I'd already seen humans did little to protect themselves. Imagine running about without a sword or long blade? What if a beast attacked?

Although, on my first day here, I was instructed to leave mine at home. I'd placed my sword in the space provided for my belongings just in case.

"Does this mean you're not avoiding me?" she said, her attention on my throat.

"Why would I do that?"

Her feet fidgeted. "Well, sometimes after a guy's been with someone, he doesn't want anything more to do with her."

"Who would do such a thing?" A growl ripped up my throat. "Has someone done this to you?"

"No. Not recently, that is. I meant we were together in the field hockey shed, but we haven't spoken since."

I stroked her cheek with the back of my hand. "You're my mate. Since you asked me to use human courtship rituals, I needed time to prepare. I apologize if that made you feel I didn't wish to fuck you again."

Her laugh snorted out. "Oh, I assumed you'd be eager for that if we got locked in another closet."

"Never fear, mate," I said. "Once I have satisfied your requirements, this will be settled."

A frown bloomed on her face.

Fortunately, the stelladon appeared to have decided it liked her since it nuzzled her arm without biting off a hunk of flesh. I could understand its eagerness to nibble on Autumn.

I couldn't wait to do the same myself.

CHAPTER 21
AUTUMN

After work, I raced home and placed my new house plant in a place of prominence—and well away from the others after it ate three leaves off my lime tree.

I dropped a hunk of chicken near its base and watching in amazement as it gobbled the meat up, then raced around my apartment, cleaning.

Thraal still liked me.

Should I put on something slinky before he got here? When he visited, I might be able to lure him into my bedroom . . .

I ate dinner and put on a sundress, something that looked cute but wasn't too suggestive.

Sitting on my back deck, I waited for him to arrive, wondering what he'd bring me tonight. His version of flowers had been quite a surprise.

When he knocked on the door, I leapt up and hurried across my living room. I swung open the door.

He was a stick of chocolate in need of licking. Well, not exactly, but he'd dressed in a t-shirt that hugged his body enough to show off his enormous orc muscles. Jeans clung to his hips and thighs. He'd even combed his hair and tugged it back, securing it with a piece of leather at his nape.

His right hand remained behind his back.

I leaned against the doorframe, trying not to melt into a puddle on the floor.

"Autumn?" he croaked. He cleared his throat and spoke in a more normal tone. "Autumn. I've come here tonight to present you with another common human courtship item."

"I see." Hopefully not another carnivorous plant.

His hand whipped out from behind his back, palm up, with his fingers curled around something.

He released his fingers. "Heart."

I gasped, staring at the actual heart lying in his hand. "What is it?"

"A heart?" Catching my wide-eyed look, he frowned. "You said heart and flowers. I have presented flowers and now a heart."

It was almost as big as his hand. Swallowing hard, I tried to smile, but it sure wasn't easy. "Where did you get it?"

"Normally, I would hunt a creature as I'm sure human males do before presenting a heart to a potential mate. I visited a butcher instead." His brow drew together. "Have I messed this up by not stalking and killing a beast, then cutting out its heart in order to present you with something fresher?"

"Oh, no, you don't *ever* need to do something like that." Please, no.

"A heart such as this is often sold along with the other parts in the supermarket. I asked for a fresh one, though I'm disappointed it's not dripping."

"Yeah, um, it's okay. No blood needed."

He thrust his hand toward me. "Here is the heart you requested."

Thankfully, I hadn't asked him to sacrifice for me. Otherwise, I might've opened the door to a fire laid out on the hall floor and him dancing around it before he gutted an unsuspecting creature.

"Thank you," I said, backing into my apartment. "You can put it . . . Why don't I get a vase?"

It was all I could think of at the moment.

He followed me inside. "A vase?"

"Yes, with water." Really not able to think straight right now, I darted into my kitchen and pulled a wide-mouth jar out from under the sink and filled it with water.

Turning, I smiled brightly at Thraal who'd followed me into the kitchen, the heart still in his hand.

"Just . . . plop it in here," I said, placing the jar on the small kitchen table.

He grunted and tried to force it sideways into the jar, but it was too wide. Turning it, he stuffed it in pointy tip down. It plopped into the water and lay on the bottom, pink water swirling around it.

At least it wasn't still beating.

"Now that I've given you heart and flowers, you'll move in with me and be my mate," he said.

"Um, that's not exactly how human dating works."

He scowled. "What do you mean? Do you need more fucking and clit sucking to convince you?"

Fucking and clit sucking were always welcome, my body shouted, but this guy was still acting much too alpha. "You need to ask, not make demands."

He frowned. "Orcs are not used to asking. We take what we need."

"That isn't how it goes with me." I wasn't sure what else to say.

"I have failed." His shoulders sagged.

"Oh, no, not at all. You—"

"My heart is not bloody or big enough. Look at it in the glass, such a puny thing. The water isn't ruby red as it should be. And my flower. It's not aggressive enough. I knew I should've purchased a bigger one."

"It's fine. I like it. It ate chicken, and I'm planning to feed it hamburger first thing tomorrow."

He shook his head and sighed. "No, I have failed. I see now why you are not willing to mate with me." Pivoting, he stalked from the kitchen and out the front door.

"Wait." I raced after him. "I'm thrilled. Amazed. Truly!"

I continued to shout down the stairwell, but he was already gone. "Thraal. Come back!"

CHAPTER 22
THRAAL

"I failed, Jarum," I told my friend as we sat on my front porch overlooking the lawn, mugs of mead on the low table beside us. "I love her and wish to be with her, but my courtship rituals have been rebuffed."

"What do you mean?" He kicked his boots up onto the railing, leaning back in the oversized lounger.

"While she seemed to enjoy receiving the stelladon, I don't believe my heart impressed her."

"Please tell me you didn't give her a real heart."

"Why wouldn't I? It was her request."

"And a stelladon?" He cringed. "Why did you give her that?"

"She asked for heart and flowers, stating these are the usual courtship gifts. I wanted to impress her and instead, I've created a mess. She'll never mate with me now. I'll have to return to the caves and request they lock me up."

"You're going into heat?" Jarum asked, his big green eyes widening.

"As expected," I said morosely. "She seemed to enjoy my fucking, and it triggered my heat. In fact, when I—"

"Whoa." Jarum held up his hand. "Too much information, friend."

"You're much more sophisticated than me. You've been here for a year where I only arrived a few weeks prior to starting my teaching job at the high school."

"Haven't you researched this online?"

"I didn't feel the need. She made it quite clear. Heart and flowers, which I gave her. But it appears that even in something as simple as this, I've made a mistake."

"She triggered your heat, though." Frowning, he lifted his mead and took a sip. "That means she's your fated mate."

"And still, she doesn't want to live with me. She doesn't want to warm my bed, and she isn't here for me to show her how much I will cherish her always."

"Back up a bit, though withhold any explicit details, if you don't mind." Humor came through in his voice, though I wasn't sure why. This was a complete tragedy. "You did sexual things with her."

"We did."

"You don't have parents to test her."

"You know they died before I came here."

"So you don't need their approval."

I shrugged.

"You just outright asked her to be your mate?" he said.

I frowned. "Asking isn't the orc way."

"Thraal, you need to know something right now about human women. They like to be asked. Consent's a big thing here."

"Why?"

He rolled his eyes.

"You know what I mean," I said. "I'm not completely lacking the clue about this."

"Clueless is the word."

"Yes, I'm not clueless. I made sure she enjoyed herself many times before—"

"Rules, Thraal. Rules. No talking about steamy details with me or anyone else for that matter, especially other guys."

"I would never share intimate things about Autumn's clit or passage with others."

"Yeah, okay." He scrunched his green face. "So you're not clueless. But did you ask her if she wanted to be your mate, or did you tell her?"

"I . . ." I pinched my eyes shut then opened them. "I told her she would move in with me immediately, that she was my mate."

"And that's where you made your mistake. I'm sure she loved your heart and your stelladon plant."

"I'm not convinced of that."

"Do a search for hearts and flowers online, and ignore the orc stuff, will you?"

"Of course."

We sipped our mead.

"What about you and Kassia?" I asked.

His smile grew. I'd never seen my friend happier. "I think she's the one."

"You'll ask her to mate?"

"My parents will want to test her, but yeah, I'm thinking seriously about it."

I smacked his arm. "I'm really happy for you, friend."

"Thanks."

We watched traffic pass on the road and continued to sip our mead.

Finally, Jarum stood. "I need to go. My dad's calling tonight, and you know how he can go on and on."

"I appreciate your help."

He finished off his mead and placed the mug back on the table. "I'm always happy to give advice. I do have a suggestion for you regarding Autumn."

"It's hopeless." I slunk lower in my seat and rubbed my chest that had turned into a big ball of ache.

"Set things up for orc courtship."

"How will that help? She's not interested in me."

"Go to her and *ask* her if she'll be your mate," he said, ignoring my plaintive sigh. "Don't *tell* her." He leapt from the top step onto the walkway and paused to turn back to face me.

"Do you truly think that'll make a difference?" I asked.

He grinned, showing off his tusks. "I believe so."

"I suppose I could try."

CHAPTER 23

AUTUMN

Friday night, I sat in my living room, staring blankly at the TV screen. With school vacation week looming, I didn't have a thing to do. I'd tried to call Kassia, and her only reply was an excited message she left while I was in the bathroom. Something about Jarum needing a favor, that she'd be away for at least the weekend.

My lucky friend.

Even Miso wasn't up for playing. For once, he wasn't trying to rip my arm apart. He lay beside me, purring while I carefully stroked him.

Someone knocked on my door.

Miso jumped and scattered, fleeing down the hall to my bedroom.

"Who's there?" I asked, rising from the couch.

"Thraal."

"What do you want?"

"You."

My breath caught. "What do you mean by that?"

"Will you open your door?"

There was no harm in that. I unlinked the chain and

turned the lock, then swung open the panel. My eyeballs popped from my head.

Thraal stood on my landing dressed in snug leather pants open on the sides like chaps, plus a fur-trimmed vest that revealed his bulging muscles.

"Are you dressed as a Viking again? Halloween's over."

"This is not a trick, but I do hope it's a treat."

"Ha. Cute one. What do you want, Thraal?" He was cold, then hot, then cold again. I wasn't sure how to take him, though I'd begun to suspect I'd take him any way I could have him.

I needed less alpha, but it would be wrong to try to change him.

"I want . . ." He swallowed. "Would you please be my mate?"

I frowned. "What does that entail?"

"Being my everything for the rest of my days. Moving into my home if you wish, which I hope you will, and standing beside me as my equal."

"Where are your alpha trademark demands?"

"I set them aside and came here to seek your consent to court you in the traditional orc manner."

"Do orcs ask their potential mates before acting?"

"I would never demand you do something you weren't eager for."

"Thraal," I breathed. "You're not acting alpha."

"I will only act alpha if you ask me to."

"Sometimes, it can be fun, especially in the bedroom."

"As for why I am here, Autumn, I'm willing to be whatever you need."

Aw. He was such a sweetie. He wasn't changing, but he was molding himself into something that still fit with what I was asking for.

"You, Thraal," I said. "I need you. And yes, I want to be your mate."

He barreled into me, sweeping me up and flinging me over his shoulder. Pivoting, he stalked through the open doorway but paused. He lowered me to my feet. "I apologize. Would you like me to carry you away and mate with you in orc tradition?"

"You know what I'd like right now, Thraal?"

He cocked his head and watched my face. "Tell me and it's yours."

I loved that my needs mattered, but there were times in a girl's life when she just wanted to be claimed.

"For now, I want you to go all orc alpha," I said. "Don't hold anything back."

With a growl, he swept me off my feet again and dropped me across his shoulder.

Rushing out into the hall, he yanked my front door closed.

"Wait. How long are we going to be gone?"

"At least a week."

"I need to . . ." I pulled my phone and called another friend, who promised to come by, collect Miso, and take him to the pet boarder. She'd also feed my plant I'd named Fluffy.

Pocketing my phone, I tapped Thraal's back. "Let's get claiming."

With a laugh, he leapt off the landing, landing on the one outside the apartment a floor below. Another bound, and he reached the first floor. He plunged through the front door and raced around the building.

I'd walked in the woods behind the parking lot a few times, but I hadn't explored far.

With his palm seated on my ass, Thraal ran down a trail. He kept going, his heart thumping heavily in his chest.

About ten minutes later, he stopped beside a big tree and looked up. One jump, and he landed on a wooden platform surrounding a treehouse. He pushed open a door and strode inside.

A bed dominated the room.

"Where did this come from?"

"I constructed it."

Wow. For me?

He lowered me onto the bed and braced himself over me. "I love you, mate. I'm going to claim you over and over for days. Will that be alright?"

I linked my arms around his shoulders. "I love you too, which means you'd better get started."

CHAPTER 24

FIRST EPILOGUE
AUTUMN

A week later, we emerged from the treehouse. He'd stocked it for the long haul, and I was grateful he had. Between grilling dinner—then having sex—and bathing in a clear river nearby—and having more sex—and lounging on the bed—with more sex—we would've starved if he hadn't.

He leapt to the ground with me in his arms.

"Mate," he said with complete satisfaction.

I had to hand it to him; he'd taken consent to heart. Although I'd more than once told him to go all alpha on me, to my body's complete delight.

"It's sad that we have to return to civilization," I said.

"Will you move in with me?"

"I want that more than anything. Miso can come with me, right?" I'd get my friend to take care of Fluffy again.

"I love you. I love Miso."

"Watch out for his claws."

"He'll behave."

Ha ha. We'd see how that went.

"When should I move in?" I asked.

"Now?"

"Okay."

Thraal spun me around, growling into my neck. "Now there's a good mate. Sweet and compliant, just the way I like her."

I poked his chest but laughed. My fear of him trying to control me had fled, replaced with an enduring love that would last multiple lifetimes. "If I told you to take me back to the bed, and I want to emphasize *told*, what would you do?"

He grinned down at me. "Take you to the bed, spread your legs, and start licking."

"We don't have to leave quite yet, do we?"

His grin widened, and he jumped back up to the treehouse.

CHAPTER 25

SECOND EPILOGUE

AUTUMN

One Year Later

"Are you sure this will not harm him?" Thraal asked.

I adjusted the light blanket over our one-month-old son, Kodish. "He'll be fine." Kodish kicked his feet and gurgled. Such a cute mix of us both from his pale green skin to my dark hair and eyes. He was big, and I believed he'd be as tall and broad as his dad.

"I'll walk with you." He pulled a blade from the sheath on his waist and brandished it, his gaze sweeping our front yard for threats.

"You really don't need that."

"Of course I do. My mate and young child are venturing out into the wild, and I must protect them."

I chuckled. "We're going to the park. Truly, there are no beasties there."

He dipped forward in a bow and reluctantly sheathed his blade. "I'll still go with you."

"I'd love to have you walk with us."

"And I'll push the carriage. You must walk slowly. If you tire or feel even the slightest twinge of pain, you'll tell me, and I'll carry you home."

"Who'll push the stroller?"

"I can do both."

This, I almost wanted to see. I leaned against him, putting my arm as far around him as I could. "Love you, Thraal. You're my favorite orc."

"This is as it should be, mate." He said it sternly, but his eyes gleamed with humor. "You're a very good mate."

I stood on tiptoe and curled my finger, urging him closer for a kiss. "And you're also a very good mate."

I hope you enjoyed Thraal & Autumn's romance.

To read Jarum & Kassia's story,
Book 2 of the Love at First Orc Series,
pick up Orc-ishly Ever After.
Kassia's about to be tested by her
new *monster*-in-law.

Not enough orcs in your life?
Check out Candy For My Orc Boss,
Book 1 in my Monsterville, USA Series,
where a one-night-stand turns into a full orc mating.

ORC-ISHLY EVER AFTER

**My fiancé's mother is a real *monster*-in-law
& she's determined to break us up.**

I've been dating an orc, Jarum, for a few months when he proposes. I hesitate before saying yes. I want to be with him, but I'm nervous about what might be expected from an orc bride. When I agree, he says we can't fully mate until his parents approve and I've completed two ancient orc marriage tests.

We love each other, so the tests will be easy, right?

We travel to the orc kingdom, where I meet his mother, who implies she doesn't think I'm good enough for her darling son. Then she begins the tests. Who would've thought impaling her in the chest with an axe would impress her?

As soon as I please Jarum's mom, he and I will be joined in wedded bliss. But one cultural blunder on my part leads to another, and I worry I can't make this work.

Can a human and an orc merge two worlds together to find their happy ever after?

Orc-ishly Ever After is Book 2 in the Love at First Orc world. Each book is standalone but it's best if read in order.

Expect size difference, plenty of spice, a monster-in-law determined to break up an engagement, an orc with a creative tongue, laugh out loud moments, marriage tests, fated mates in heat, and a happy ever after.

Get Orc-ishly Ever After NOW!

About the Author

Ava Ross is a two-time *USA Today* Bestselling author who has written numerous titles, all of them featuring sweet and steamy romance. She fell for men with unusual features when she first watched Star Wars, where alien creatures have gone mainstream. She lives in New England with her husband (who is sadly not an alien, though he is still cute in his own way), her kids, and a few assorted pets.